P9-CFW-023

SCOOBY-DOO!™
AND THE
Thanksgiving Terror

by Mariah Balaban

SCHOLASTIC INC.

New York   Toronto   London   Auckland   Sydney
Mexico City   New Delhi   Hong Kong   Buenos Aires

No part of this publication may be reproduced, stored in a retrieval system, or transmitted in any form or by any means, electronic, mechanical, photocopying, recording, or otherwise, without written permission of the publisher. For information regarding permission, write to Scholastic Inc., Attention: Permissions Department, 557 Broadway, New York, NY 10012.

ISBN 13: 978-0-545-08076-7
ISBN 10: 0-545-08076-2

Copyright © 2008 Hanna-Barbera.

SCOOBY-DOO and all related characters and elements are trademarks of and © Hanna-Barbera.

Published by Scholastic Inc. All rights reserved.

SCHOLASTIC and associated logos are trademarks and/or registered trademarks of Scholastic Inc.

Designed by Michael Massen

12   11   10   9   8   7   6   5   4   3   2   10 11 12 13 14/0

Printed in the U.S.A.   40

First printing, September 2008

It was Thanksgiving, and the Mystery, Inc. gang was going to have their very own float in the Gladcash's Thanksgiving Day Parade.

"I'm so excited!" said Daphne. "This is such a big honor! Gladcash's Department Store is the biggest, most important store in Coolsville!"

"So what is Wallbucks, chopped liver?" asked a little man who had been standing next to the gang.

"Like, who are you, the Earl of Sandwich?" giggled Shaggy.

"I'm Wally Wallbucks!" he said. "And Wallbucks's Department Store is every bit as good as Gladcash's. One of these days I'll settle the score, just you wait and see!"

"Jeepers!" exclaimed Velma. "He sure seemed angry!"

It was almost time for the parade to start, so the gang made their way to the floats.

"Hey, isn't that the pop star Simone Chantay?" asked Fred.

Simone Chantay wasn't very happy with Hugo Gladcash either. "Who does that Hugo Gladcash think he is, making me share my float with a bunch of bears!" they heard Simone Chantay yell. "No one treats a star this way and gets away with it! I'll make Gladcash pay!"

GLADCASH

"Like, that pop star's flipped her lid!" said Shaggy.

Suddenly two men ran by. They were so busy arguing that they almost knocked Velma over.

"Studder, you're FIRED!" yelled one of the men. "Get off the parade grounds!"

"You haven't seen the last of Stu Studder," the other man yelled back. "Hugo Gladcash and his stupid department store are going down!"

"We'd better get over to our float," said Fred. "It looks like the parade is about to start."

"Welcome to the fiftieth annual Gladcash's Thanksgiving Day Parade!" Hugo Gladcash announced over a loudspeaker.

"It sure is fun to be a part of all this," said Fred as he waved to the cheering crowd.

Suddenly the cheers turned to screams.

"I didn't think our float was that scary!" said Shaggy.

"Shaggy, behind you!" exclaimed Daphne. "It's, it's . . ."

"A giant turkey!" Fred screamed.

Fred was right! A giant turkey balloon had broken free from its handlers and was bouncing through the crowd.

"I'm the Thanksgiving Terror," it squawked. "I'll use you for stuffing and cook your goose!"

"That terrible turkey is chasing everyone away from the parade!" exclaimed Velma.

"I can't hear you," cried Shaggy. "Like, I'm too busy running!"

"Re, roo!" said Scooby-Doo.

The Thanksgiving Terror disappeared around the corner, and the gang came back to look for Mr. Gladcash. They found him among the empty floats.

"My parade was a disaster!" Mr. Gladcash cried. "I'm ruined! Who could have done this?"

"Don't worry, Mr. Gladcash, we'll get to the bottom of this mystery," Velma reassured him.

"Gang, let's split up and look for clues," said Fred.

"Like, I was afraid he would say that," groaned Shaggy.

While Velma, Fred, and Daphne explored the parade stands, Shaggy and Scooby explored the snack table.

"Now these are the kinds of clues we're happy to look for, right, Scoob?" Shaggy asked.

"Rurkey!" yelped Scooby-Doo.

"No thanks, buddy," Shaggy replied. "I think I've had enough turkey for one day."

"Raggy, rehind roo!" said Scooby.

Shaggy turned around slowly. Something had tapped him on the shoulder. It was hard and pointy . . . like a beak.

"But it wouldn't be Thanksgiving without the turkey," said the Thanksgiving Terror.

"Like, sorry, big guy, nothing personal," Shaggy gulped. "Scooby-Doo, let's run for it!"

Meanwhile, Fred, Daphne, and Velma were busy looking for clues.

"I found something, guys!" exclaimed Daphne.

Daphne picked up a walking stick with a big "W" on it and showed it to the gang.

"I bet that belongs to Wally Wallbucks," said Fred.

"Hmm . . . " thought Velma aloud. "This could just be a coincidence, but Wally Wallbucks was acting awfully suspicious before."

The gang decided to keep looking for clues. Over by the parade floats, the gang found some more.

"That's Simone Chantay's signature beret," said Daphne.

"And this must be Stu Studder's employee jacket!" exclaimed Fred.

"This mystery is finally coming together," said Velma. "But where are Scooby and Shaggy?"

"Man, like, it looks like we finally lost that overstuffed entrée!" Shaggy gasped.

"Rook again, Raggy!" said Scooby.

"You can run, but you can't hide! Your giblets are goners!" squawked the terrifying turkey as it came for them.

Shaggy and Scooby ran into the rest of the gang with a loud clatter. They had crashed into a bunch of helium canisters stashed behind the floats.

"That helium must be how the Thanksgiving Terror stays inflated," said Velma.

"Those helium canisters and this parade float just gave me an idea for a trap," said Fred.

Fred instructed Mr. Gladcash to make an announcement over the loudspeaker.

"Ladies and gentlemen," said Mr. Gladcash, "that giant turkey was part of the festivities. Please return to the stands so that the parade can continue."

Soon the crowd had returned, and the parade started up again. This time, with a special float leading it.

As Scooby and Shaggy waved to the crowd, they noticed a big, turkey-shaped shadow looming behind them.

The Thanksgiving Terror had come back, just as Fred had counted on.

"Gobble, gobble, you're all in trouble," squawked the giant bird.

"Shaggy, *now!*" Fred shouted.

Right on Fred's cue, Shaggy thrust his pitchfork into the Thanksgiving Terror. With a loud *POP!*, the balloon ripped, and the air rushed out of it.

Everyone cheered as the enormous turkey flapped uncontrollably around the parade.

"Now it's time to see who's behind this bird-brained mystery!" exclaimed Fred as he pulled off the turkey's head.

"Stu Studder!" exclaimed Mr. Gladcash. "But why?"

"Stu tried to sabotage the parade because he was angry for being fired," explained Velma.

"Fired?" asked Mr. Gladcash. "Why? Because of Stu, my parade is more popular than ever! Plus, these turkey souvenirs are selling like hotcakes!"

"Does that mean I have my job back?" Stu Studder asked.

"Young man, I'm giving you a promotion!" exclaimed Mr. Gladcash. "And it's all thanks to Scooby-Doo and his friends! Now, who's hungry?"

"Like, I think that's a trick question," Shaggy whispered to Scooby.

Mr. Gladcash invited the gang to join him at a special Thanksgiving feast hosted by Gladcash's department store. "Like, I never thought I'd say this, but can somebody please pass the turkey?" Shaggy joked. Everyone laughed. "Rappy Ranksriving!" barked Scooby-Doo.